Knight

Steve Barlow and Steve Skidmore

Illustrated by Judit Tondora

Franklin Watts
First published in Great Britain in 2019 by The Watts Publishing Group

Text © Steve Barlow and Steve Skidmore 2019
Illustrations by Judit Tondora © Franklin Watts 2019
The "2Steves" illustration by Paul Davidson
used by kind permission of Orchard Books

PB ISBN 978 1 4451 6957 6
ebook ISBN 978 1 4451 6959 0
Library ebook ISBN 978 1 4451 6958 3

1 3 5 7 9 10 8 6 4 2

Printed in Great Britain

Franklin Watts
An imprint of
Hachette Children's Group
Part of The Watts Publishing Group
Carmelite House
50 Victoria Embankment
London EC4Y 0DZ

An Hachette UK Company
www.hachette.co.uk

www.franklinwatts.co.uk

How to be a hero

This book is not like others you have read.
This is a choose-your-own-destiny book
where YOU are the hero of this adventure.

Each section of this book is numbered.
At the end of most sections, you will have
to make a choice. Each choice will take you
to a different section of the book.

If you choose correctly, you will succeed.
But be careful. If you make a bad choice,
you may have to start the adventure again.
If this happens, make sure you learn from
your mistake!

Go to the next page to start your
adventure. And remember, don't be a zero,
be a hero!

You are one of the Knights of the Round Table. You serve Arthur, King of the Britons. You have fought many battles, defending Arthur's kingdom against its enemies.

You are known for your bravery and chivalrous nature.

One midwinter morning, you are called to the Great Hall in the castle of Camelot. You take your place at the Round Table. The other knights are present, but there is no sign of the king.

Arthur's magician, Merlin, enters the hall looking worried.

"I have grave news concerning the king," he says. "Arthur has been captured by the sorceress, Morgan Le Fay..."

Go to 1.

1

"How did this happen?" you ask.

"Morgan sent a message saying that the queen had suffered a riding accident. Arthur hurried into the forest but it was a trap and he was taken prisoner.

"Morgan is demanding that she is named as the rightful ruler of the kingdom otherwise she will kill the king…"

"Where is the king being kept?" you ask.

"I do not know," replies Merlin. "I have tried to discover this, but Morgan is a powerful enchantress. She is using a hex that stops me locating his whereabouts."

Lancelot leaps up from his seat.

"Then we shall find Morgan and rescue our king!" He storms out of the hall.

"Wait, I need to say more on this matter," says Merlin, but the other knights ignore him and follow Lancelot.

If you wish to listen to what Merlin has to say, go to 49.

If you wish to join the knights, go to 25.

2

You open the door. "Who is there?" you ask.

"It is me, Arthur!"

"My king," you say and step inside.

BOOM! The door slams shut behind you and laughter fills the dungeon.

"Welcome to the rest of your life. You will rot here!"

There is no one in the dungeon but you!

You made a big mistake! Go to 17.

3

You urge your horse down an earth track. The dense trees cut out most of the sunlight and you realise why the forest is so named.

After some time you reach a clearing with a pool. Three young women sit at its edge, laughing. They see you and one calls out, "Come and join us, brave knight."

To stop and talk, go to 23.

If you don't think you have time to stop, go to 34.

4

You pull the lance from the ground and steady it under your arm.

You urge your horse into a full charge, bringing you closer and closer to your oncoming opponent. You aim your lance at the knight's shield and ready yourself for the impact.

Suddenly, your lance disintegrates into dust! You have been fooled.

There is no time to avoid the black knight's lance. It smashes into you, propelling you out of the saddle and onto the hard ground. You lie on the earth as the black knight clambers from his horse.

Taking out his sword he stands above you.

"Yield!" he says. "And pay homage to my mistress!"

"Never!" you cry.

Go to 17.

5

You spur your horse down the pathway.
The light from the glow-worms is dazzling.

Suddenly, the air is filled with the beating
of wings. Attracted by the light, thousands of
giant moths swarm around you.

Startled by the moths, your horse rears
up and you are thrown to the ground. Your
head smashes against the hard forest floor
and you pass out.

Go to 22.

6

After many hours of travelling you arrive
at a mighty river that stands between you
and the Purple Mountains. A wooden bridge
spans the raging water.

A young child sits on the ground next to
the bridge. She sees you approaching and
jumps up.

"Give me a gold coin and I will tell you
how to cross the river," she says.

To give her a coin, go to 30.

To refuse, go to 20.

"Never!" you cry. "Now release my king or else you will pay for your foul deeds!"

You press your sword against the enchantress's neck.

"Very well!" cries Morgan. "You have won for now, but I will return and be ruler of this land!"

As Arthur's chains dissolve, the castle walls begin to come apart. With a squawk, Morgan transforms into a crow and flies away.

Blocks of stone crash down around you as the castle collapses.

"My Lord, follow me," you cry as you run towards your horse. You and the king leap on its back.

You spur the horse past the falling masonry and through the gates to safety as the castle sinks into the lake forever.

Go to 50.

8

As the ropes are cut you leap forward and grab hold of your sword. But before you can use it, the second troll brings his wooden club down onto your arm.

You drop the sword and fall to the ground. The troll raises his weapon above your head. You have to move quickly!

Go to 17.

9

You continue along the forest path. Day turns into night and you can hardly see ahead. Howls and shrieks ring through the forest.

You feel your horse tremble as its ears prick up. It comes to a sudden halt and paws at the ground.

To stop and wait for daylight, go to 28.

To urge your horse on, go to 40.

10

You take one of the lit torches and swing it at the bats. The flames stop the creatures from getting near you and you retreat through the doors, slamming them shut.

Making your way back to the courtyard, you suddenly stop in horror. A dragon stands before you!

To talk to the dragon, go to 47.

To attack it, go to 38.

13

You drop your sword and the air glistens with stars as the dragon melts away. The intense light dies away to reveal Morgan Le Fay standing before you.

Kneeling next to her is King Arthur, chained and guarded by an ogre.

"You have shown your bravery," says Morgan. "And so I will make you an offer. Renounce Arthur and you will rule the land with me..."

To accept Morgan's offer, go to 21.

To attack Morgan, go to 41.

To attack the ogre and try to free Arthur, go to 31.

"It seems you know of my quest," you say. "Who are you?"

"We are sisters of the Lady of the Lake," the lady replies. "We wish to tell you that Merlin has sent his birds across the land to seek Morgan's whereabouts. He will send word to you when he discovers it. In the meantime, continue through the Dark Forest."

You bow. "Thank you for your help."

"One final word of warning," says the eldest. "People and beasts are not what they seem! Morgan is a powerful enchantress and can disguise what is and isn't real. Trust in your heart to know their true identities."

As if to prove her point, the air is suddenly a whirlwind of noise as the three sisters transform into swans. With a beat of their wings they take to the sky, leaving you to continue your journey.

Go to 9.

"My quarrel is not with you," you reply. "I seek your mistress."

You leave the knight stranded on the ground and ride across the stone bridge into the castle.

You are surprised to find that the gate is open and there are no guards protecting the entrance.

In fact, the whole castle seems deserted. The clatter of your horse's hooves on the paved courtyard echoes eerily in the silence.

This is strange, you think. *Why is there no one guarding the castle? Is Morgan's magic at work here?*

You dismount your horse and wonder what to do next.

To head for the Great Hall, go to 24.

To head for the dungeons, go to 33.

16

The troll warily hands back your sword.

"Thank you," you say. "And where is my horse?"

"We were er... keeping it safe for you," grunts one of the trolls. "It's standing outside our cave."

They take you to the cave and you mount the horse.

"Thank you for your help... One final question, where will I find the Lady Morgan?"

The trolls look at each other. One shakes his head. The other nods and replies. "She's er... she's at the Castle of the Black Peak, to the east of the forest."

"Thank you and farewell." You spur your horse on.

If you believe the trolls, go to 43.

If you don't, go to 39.

You take hold of Merlin's amulet and cry, "Lady of the Lake, help me!"

There is a roaring of wind and a kaleidoscope of colour as you pass through time and space.

You find yourself back in the Great Hall of Camelot. It is strangely quiet and deserted with all your fellow knights away on their quest to find Arthur.

Merlin stands before you, scowling.

"All my magic cannot help you make the right decisions," he says. "You chose wrongly, and so you must begin your quest again."

Once more your squire saddles your horse and you ride out of Camelot.

To head to the Purple Mountains, go to 6.

To head to the Dark Forest, go to 37.

18

It is late afternoon when you finally emerge from the depths of the Dark Forest.

A deep blue lake lies before you with Morgan Le Fay's castle by its edge. A stone bridge leads the way into the castle.

Before you can reach it, a clatter of hooves sounds out. A horse, bearing a knight dressed in black armour, gallops over the bridge.

The knight holds two lances and throws one towards you. It embeds itself in the ground.

His voice rings out. "I challenge you! To cross this bridge you will have to fight me!"

To choose to fight with your sword, go to 42.

To choose the lance, go to 4.

19

This is all too easy, you think. You recall the words of the three sisters: *"People and beasts are not what they seem! Trust in your heart to know their true identities."*

"Hurry and release me," says Arthur.

To do as he says, go to 44.

To question him, go to 35.

20

"There is a bridge here and I will use it!" you say.

You urge your horse onto the bridge.

There is an ear-splitting howl behind you. You turn to see the child transforming into a hideous ogre.

"My mistress Morgan says, 'Farewell!'" She takes an axe and chops at the ropes holding the bridge.

You fall from your horse and plunge into the river. Your heavy armour pulls you down into the raging torrent.

Go to 17.

You look at your defeated king and consider Morgan's offer. To rule the country with her!

"Very well, I accept," you say. "I renounce Arthur!"

She laughs! "You have no honour! You are a traitor and there is only one fate for traitors!"

"Arthur" transforms into a huge bear. With a strike of its gigantic paw, you are smashed to the ground.

Go to 17.

22

When you wake up, your head is throbbing and your body aches all over. After a moment, you realise that you cannot move — you are tied to a tree! Your horse is nowhere in sight but standing a few metres away are a pair of forest trolls. They have their backs to you. One holds your sword.

"Well, I say we eat him. He'll make a fine meal!" he says.

"And I say we should deliver him to Mistress Morgan," replies the other, "just as we did with the last knight that came into the forest. She will reward us greatly!"

To try and reach your amulet, go to 48.

To try and break free of your bonds, go to 11.

To talk to the trolls, go to 45.

23

You dismount your horse and move cautiously towards the group.

"We hear you seek Morgan Le Fay," says the eldest of the group.

"How do you know this?" you ask.

"We know many things that are not for your ears," she replies.

To try and force them to tell you more, go to 46.

To ask for their help, go to 14.

To carry on with your quest, go to 43.

24

If Morgan is here, surely she wouldn't be in a dungeon? you think.

You head into the heart of the castle. Before you is a set of huge wooden doors.

You fling the doors open to see a hall lit by flaming torches and revealing King Arthur, standing in chains before you.

To release Arthur immediately, go to 44.

To investigate the hall, go to 19.

25

Before you can leave the hall, Merlin steps in front of you.

He holds out a hand to stop your hurried departure.

"Good knight, do not be hot-headed like Lancelot. I have more to tell about this sorry business."

You realise Merlin is right. You need more information.

Go to 49.

26

With a roar, you rush towards the dragon, but despite its size it moves with incredible speed, swatting you away with its wing.

You fly through the air and crash against a wall before falling to the ground where you lie winded and helpless.

The dragon stalks towards you and opens its mouth, ready to blast you with a sheet of fire.

Go to 17.

27

You bring your horse to a halt.

"I have news from Merlin," says the raven. "It is as he suspected — Morgan Le Fay is at the Castle of the Blue Lake. The other Knights of the Round Table are many miles from the castle. Arthur's rescue is in your hands alone. You must make haste."

The raven flies off and you spur your horse forward. Time is running out!

Go to 18.

28

You dismount and secure your horse. You make a bed of leaves and branches and settle down for the night.

However, the noise of the forest keeps you on your guard and you get little sleep. Dawn finally breaks — you have survived the night!

Go to 43.

29

You swing your sword at the creatures, but there are too many of them to fight!

Go to 17.

30

"Very well," you say. You take out a coin and give it to her.

"If I were you I would not cross here," she says.

"For a gold coin, that is all you tell me?" you say.

She smiles. "That is all."

To ignore her advice, go to 20.

To take her advice, go to 12.

31

You snatch up your sword and charge at the ogre.

The creature swings its axe at you, but you easily avoid it. The ogre continues to fight, but your speed is too great and with a final swing you bring it to the ground.

You turn back to challenge Morgan, but the courtyard is deserted! You spend hours searching the castle for the sorceress and your king, but find nothing. They have vanished! You have failed to rescue Arthur and know there is only one thing to do.

Go to 17.

32

You take the right-hand fork and spur your horse on.

The darkness is overwhelming. Thorns and branches scratch your face and catch at your cloak.

To return to the left-hand fork, go to 5.

To stop and wait until day break, go to 28.

Drawing your sword, you make your way to the guardhouse and down the stone stairs that lead to the dungeons.

"Help me!" Your heart misses a beat as a cry echoes around the stairwell.

"Help me!" You hear the cries coming from behind a closed iron door. "Help me!"

You pause. A shiver passes through your body. Something doesn't feel quite right.

To open the door, go to 2.

To go back and head for the Great Hall, go to 24.

34

"I have no time to idle away, I am on an important quest," you say.

"We know that you seek King Arthur," says one of the group.

You wonder how they know of your quest.

To talk to them, go to 23.

To force them to tell you how they know, go to 46.

To continue your journey, go to 43.

35

"Are you truly my king?" you ask.

"Of course."

"Then say who I am..."

The figure doesn't reply but instead gives out a strange high-pitched squeal.

This is not Arthur!

There is a crash of thunder and "Arthur" transforms into a swarm of bats. They bite and scratch with their teeth and claws.

To fight with your sword, go to 29.

To use the flaming torches, go to 10.

"Very well," you say.

You dismount your horse and approach the fallen man. But as you raise your sword, there is a sudden blast of wind. The air swirls as the knight transforms into a huge black serpent! In a flash, the creature coils its body around you, crushing your body in a vice-like grip.

You try to break free but it is useless.

Go to 17.

37

After many miles of hard riding, you reach the edge of the Dark Forest. It looks forbidding. The trees are gnarled and twisted into strange shapes; their leaves are pale and spotted with disease. No birds sing.

You hear howling and strange cries coming from within the depths of the forest.

To head around the forest, go to 43.

To go through the forest, go 3.

38

You charge at the dragon but before you can get near enough to use your sword, the creature shoots a river of fire at you.

You feel the blistering heat even through your armour as you dive out of the way, narrowly avoiding the deadly flames.

To continue the attack, go to 26.

To talk to the dragon, go to 47.

39

From their manner, you know that the trolls were lying to you, so you continue your journey northwards through the forest.

After hours of riding, you hear a voice calling out, "Good knight, listen to me!"

You look up to see a raven sitting on a branch. It is speaking to you.

What magic is this? you wonder.

To ignore it, go to 43.

To listen to it, go to 27.

You pat your horse's neck. "Be brave,"
you say.

Your reassuring manner calms the beast
and you continue on your way.

Soon you come across a fork in the path.
The path to the right is dark and forbidding.
You look to your left and are amazed to see
a strange white glow lighting up the way.

"Glow-worms!" you whisper.

To take the left fork, go to 5.

To take the right fork, go to 32.

"Never!" you cry. Snatching up your sword you charge at Morgan Le Fay.

The ogre tries to stop you, but you slash at its legs and it falls to the ground.

Before Morgan can summon up a spell, you place your sword against her neck.

"Release my king," you say.

"But you can be my king," she replies. "My offer still stands..."

To accept her offer, go to 21.

To refuse her offer, go to 7.

Your instinct tells you not to trust the knight.

"I will make battle with my sword," you say.

"Very well!"

With a cry, the knight spurs his horse forward. You respond and urge your horse on.

Just as your opponent is about to strike, you pull your horse hard to the right.

The Black Knight's lance misses you by a hair's breadth. You pull back on the reins, swing your sword and score a hit on the knight's back with the flat of the blade.

The blow causes him to lose his balance. He topples from his saddle and crashes to the ground. The weight of his armour keeps him pinned down and you climb from your horse.

Standing over the knight, you point your sword at his chest.

"End it," he says. "I have lost my honour."

To do as the knight says, go to 36.

To refuse his request, go to 15.

45

"Greetings!" you say. The trolls look at you with murderous eyes. "I fell from my horse. Thank you for taking care of me!" you say.

The trolls look puzzled. "You do know we are thinking of eating you?"

You laugh. "Well, that wouldn't do! I carry an important message for Morgan Le Fay, so I'm sure she wouldn't approve!"

"We'd better let him go," says the troll holding your sword, and he cuts you free.

To attack the trolls, go to 8.

To ride away, go to 16.

46

You take out your sword. "Tell me what you know or it will be all the worse for you!"

"Such behaviour makes you unworthy of our help," snaps one of the group.

There is a rush of air as the women transform into huge white swans and attack you. Their beating wings and snapping beaks overpower you.

Go to 17.

You stand before the dragon. "I do not believe you are what you appear to be," you say.

The dragon laughs. "Then face me without a weapon, or are you not brave enough to do that?"

To drop your sword, go to 13.

To attack the dragon, go to 26.

48

You try to reach for the amulet, but the rope holding you is too tight. You can't rely on magic to get you out of this situation!

To try and break free of your bonds, go to 11.

To talk to the trolls, go to 45.

49

"What else should I know?" you ask.

"It is possible that Morgan has taken Arthur to the Castle of the Blue Lake, in the wilds of the North," says Merlin. "The ways to the castle are many but the quickest by far are through the Dark Forest or across the Purple Mountains. Both paths are fraught with danger."

"I will risk all for the king," you reply.

Merlin smiles and hands you an amulet.

"This is my magical birthstone, given to me by the Lady of the Lake. If you find yourself in jeopardy, take hold of it and call upon the power of the Lady.

"You will find yourself back in this time and place, unharmed and ready to restart your quest."

You hang the amulet around your neck. "Thank you, Merlin. And now I must leave and search for the good king."

Your squire saddles your horse and hands you your sword. You ride out of Camelot determined to find Morgan.

To head to the Purple Mountains, go to 6.

To head to the Dark Forest, go to 37.

50

When you arrive back at Camelot, the
Knights of the Round Table cheer as you
enter the Great Hall in triumph. Merlin
and the queen stand and applaud.

Arthur takes your hand and holds it aloft.
He addresses the gathered knights.

"You are all brave knights, but truly,
this knight is the bravest of them all.
The kingdom is saved!" King Arthur turns
to you and smiles. "You are a true hero!"

Immortals

I HERO Quiz

Test yourself with this special quiz. It has been designed to see how much you remember about the book you've just read. Can you get all five answers right?

Question 1

Where do you meet Merlin at the start of the adventure?

A   Castle of Camelot

B   Purple Mountains

C   Castle of the Blue Lake

D   Dark Forest

Question 2

Where do you eventually find Arthur?

A   the forest

B   the Castle of the Blue Lake

C   the mountains

D   in a cave

Question 3

What creatures do the three women transform into?

A   deer

B   parrots

C   trolls

D   swans

Question 4

What is your mission?

A   capture Morgan Le Fay

B   kill King Arthur

C   rescue your king

D   destroy the Purple Mountains

Question 5

What did Morgan Le Fay want to do?

A   make war between two lands

B   find Merlin's amulet

C   destroy the people of Camelot

D   rule the land

Answers:
1. A; 2. B; 3. D; 4. C and 5. D.

About the 2Steves

"The 2Steves" are one of Britain's most popular writing double acts for young people, specialising in comedy and adventure. They perform regularly in schools and libraries, and at festivals, taking the power of words and story to audiences of all ages.

Together they have written many books, including the *Monster Hunter* series. Find out what they've been up to at: **www.the2steves.net**

About the illustrator: Judit Tondora

Judit Tondora was born in Miskolc, Hungary and now works from her countryside studio. Judit's artwork has appeared in books, comics, posters and on commercial design projects.

To find out more about her work, visit: **www.astound.us/publishing/artists/ judit-tondora**